When The Pixels Fade

Dedication

To the Almighty, the eternal source of light and love, who guides my path in silence and grace.

To all my beloved ones. The ones who hold space for my silences, who remind me of my worth when I forget, and love me not through pixels, but presence.

And to this fast, loud, endlessly wired society, may we learn to slow down, to see one another with gentler eyes, and to return to what is real, what is true.

With unwavering gratitude and all my heart,
— *Arghyaraj Basu*

About the Author

Arghyaraj Basu is an advocate by profession and a seeker by spirit. Beyond the courtroom, his passion lies in exploring the quiet, often overlooked spaces of the human experience presence, stillness, connection, and meaning.

He is the author of two previous books, *Awaken Through Karma and Stillness in the Storm,* both of which invite readers to reflect inward and journey toward personal truth. With, When the Pixel Fades, Arghyaraj shifts his voice toward fiction, weaving a deeply human story about digital life, disconnection, and the healing found in real-world presence.

Whether through the written word or spoken truth, his work continues to ask the same quiet, powerful question:

What happens when we finally come home to ourselves?

Author's Note

This story began in the quiet. Not on a screen. Not with a notification.

But in one of those rare, still moments when I realized how loud the world had become and how easy it was to lose myself in it.

When the Pixel Fades is fiction, but it's also deeply personal. Like Mira, I've felt the pull of the scroll, the ache of invisible comparison, the comfort of being constantly "connected" while feeling more alone than ever. This book grew from questions I've wrestled with about identity, attention, presence, and what it means to really be here, without the buffer of a screen.

If you've ever felt that ache… you're not alone. And you're not broken.

You're just human in a hyperconnected world that never really taught us how to unplug, to slow down, or to sit with silence. But those things those old, analog ways of being they still live inside us. They're just waiting to be remembered.

This story is my reminder to myself. And maybe now, it's one for you, too.

To anyone reading this: thank you. For pausing. For turning pages instead of swiping. For being present with Mira and maybe, with yourself.

I hope you take what you need from these chapters.

And I hope you give yourself permission to unplug, even just for a moment.

The world will still be there. But so will you.

With love,

— Arghyaraj Basu

CONTENTS

Chapter 1: Wake, Scroll, Repeat

The first thing Mira noticed when she woke up wasn't the time. It was the quiet. The kind that clings to early morning, where everything still feels a little too far away to touch.

Her phone was under her pillow, still warm from being there all night.

She checked the screen like a reflex.
6:32 a.m. No new texts. Two likes on last night's story.
A small part of her felt… disappointed.

She told herself she didn't care, but her chest disagreed.

Swipe. Open. Scroll.

Mira moved through the feed slowly this morning, not because she was tired, she was always tired but because the scrolling gave her something her thoughts didn't: noise.

Her own mind was quiet in a way that felt dangerous. Like a room you weren't supposed to be alone in.

There were memes. Videos. A girl doing a morning routine with a voice-over that said, "Romanticize your life, babe." Mira paused on that one. The girl had fairy lights and a latte. Mira had crusty eyes and a math test.

She flipped the phone over and stared at the ceiling.

"I used to wake up and write in a journal," she muttered to herself. "What happened to her?"

She already knew the answer. That version of her the one who filled notebooks with stories and doodles got smaller every time she reached for the screen instead of the page.

Downstairs, her mom was cooking eggs and humming something old from the radio.

Mira took one look at the food and mumbled, "Not hungry," grabbing a granola bar instead.

"You haven't eaten a real breakfast all week," her mom said, not unkindly.

“I’m fine,” Mira replied, too quickly. She unwrapped the bar and turned toward the door, chewing before she could be asked anything else.

Outside, the day was already buzzing. School, deadlines, notifications, unspoken rules.

Her phone buzzed in her pocket like a tiny, demanding animal.

At school, Mira floated through her classes like a ghost draped in denim and earbuds. People said hi, but not in ways that meant anything. She responded with half-smiles.

She didn’t mind being alone. She just hated how alone it felt.

At lunch, she sat at the edge of a group she used to belong to. They were too busy showing each other Instagram to notice. Mira smiled once, genuinely, when someone played an old Vine clip she used to love. But when she laughed, it sounded like someone else’s voice.

Later, in chemistry, she caught herself staring at the window more than the board.

There was a tree outside, shedding leaves like secrets.

She opened her Notes app and typed:

She looked at it for a while. Didn't post it. Just saved it and locked her phone.

It was one of the first times all day she felt real.

That night, Mira curled up in bed with her phone an inch from her nose, screen brightness down, heart turned up.

She scrolled for hours, looking for something she couldn't name. She liked posts she didn't care about. Replied to DMs she didn't feel connected to. Watched a reel of someone crying and wondered why it felt more honest than her own conversations.

The glow from the screen painted her face in blue and white.

Eventually, she opened her camera, stared at herself.

Not ugly. Not beautiful. Just… blurred. Like she wasn't fully there.

She closed her eyes. The screen stayed on, lighting the dark even after she stopped watching.

Chapter 2: Filters and Fractures

Mira didn't hate school. She just didn't see the point of being somewhere if no one actually looked at each other.

The hallways buzzed with noise, but none of it felt alive. Everyone walked with their heads tilted downward, eyes fixed on their screens, fingers flying like insects. There were entire conversations happening in silence a raised brow at a text, a low laugh from a meme, a group chat blowing up with inside jokes no one said out loud.

Mira moved through it all like wallpaper seen, but not noticed.

She leaned against her locker, checking her phone. New DM: "u, okay? u looked sad today lol." From someone she hadn't spoken to in person since October.

She didn't reply. Just locked her phone and let her head thud lightly against the cool metal.

In English class, Ms. Rivera was trying to lead a discussion on Fahrenheit 451, but only three people had done the reading. Mira had sort of. She skimmed a summary online this morning.

Still, she liked the sound of it: books being outlawed, people losing the ability to think for themselves, distracted by endless screens.

She glanced around the room. The irony was so loud it could've knocked her out of her chair.

Ms. Rivera paced slowly in front of the whiteboard; eyes tired but determined. "Bradbury wasn't predicting a world where books are banned because of censorship. He was warning us about distraction. Constant, numbing distraction. Sound familiar?"

Silence.

Mira stared down at her desk, doodling stars in the corner of her notebook. A quiet voice interrupted her scribbles.

"You ever think we're already there?" someone said.

She looked up. A guy near the back. Hoodie. Messy hair. A sketchpad opens in front of him instead of a laptop. He hadn't said anything in class all year.

Ms. Rivera paused. “Go on, Evan.”

Evan shrugged. “I mean, people don’t even look at the sky anymore. They Google it.”

A few students chuckled. Ms. Rivera smiled the real kind.

Mira blinked. She hadn’t noticed Evan before, but now she couldn’t not notice him.

After class, she lingered by the door, pretending to text.

Evan walked past without a word; sketchpad tucked under one arm.

Mira watched him go.

At lunch, her old friend group sat in a circle like always ten feet apart, yet somewhere even further. Kyla was crying over a comment someone left on her post. Reese was live-streaming himself eating hot Cheetos for some reason. The rest were laughing about a viral challenge Mira didn’t understand.

She sat with them, but didn't speak.

Not because she had nothing to say. Just… nothing that mattered in that moment.

She scrolled. Liked. Watched.

But her heart didn't move.

She opened her Notes app again:

Is it possible to be surrounded and still starve?

She saved it. Locked her phone. Bit into her apple and stared at the clouds.
They were still moving. Even if no one looked up.
Later that night, the house was still. Her mom had gone to bed early. Mira lay in bed, surrounded by the soft hum of electronics. Phone charging. Laptop fan whirring. Router lights blinking in the corner of the room like miniature lighthouses.
She opened an old note from months ago a half-written poem she never finished.
Mira closed the app. Her fingers hovered over Instagram. She clicked it out of habit.
But it didn't open.
A spinning wheel.
Then a message: "No internet connection."

She frowned. Checked her Wi-Fi. Nothing. She reached for her laptop. No signal. The router was still blinking green, red, red.
Weird.

She turned on the TV. Black screen.

Then her bedroom light flickered.
Went out.
Complete darkness.
She sat up fast, heart picking up pace. Her phone still had some charge, but no bars. No service. No internet. No anything.
The silence was instant.
Too still. Too deep.
She sat there, holding her phone like a lifeline that had suddenly gone limp.
It was just a blackout.
Right?

Chapter 3: The Blackout

The house had never felt this quiet.

No fridge hums. No heating clicks. No distant sounds from the neighbors 'TVs. Just a dense, unnatural stillness that seemed to press in from the corners of the walls.
Mira sat on her bed, her phone clutched in both hands like it might wake up if she held it tight enough.
Still nothing.
No signal. No Wi-Fi. No service.
She opened and closed apps, toggled airplane mode on and off, even restarted the phone twice. The screen came back to life each time, but it was like shouting into a void. The world beyond her walls had gone dark.
She went downstairs.
The hallway was dim, lit only by a sliver of moonlight slipping through the kitchen blinds. Her mom's voice floated in from the living room.

"Nothing's working," she said, fiddling with the TV remote. "Not even the landline."

"Landline?" Mira echoed. "Who even uses that?"
Her mom shot her a look. "Maybe people who remember what life was like before Google."

"Cool," Mira muttered, folding her arms. "So… is this, like, a storm thing? Or a system crash? Or…?"
Her mom shrugged. "The power company's not answering. My guess? City-wide outage."
"How long?" Mira asked, too quickly.
Her mom gave her a tired smile. "You'll survive a few hours without Instagram, sweetheart."
Mira didn't smile back.
It wasn't about Instagram. Not really.

It was about the everything that lived inside the screen: conversations, news, music, escape. Her lifeline. Her anchor. Her entire way of feeling less alone.
By 1 a.m., the silence had teeth.

Mira tried everything watching saved videos, rereading old texts, scrolling through her camera roll like a security blanket. But even those started to feel hollow. Without new input, it was just… noise she'd already memorized.

Her hands were twitchy. Restless. Like her body expected stimulation that wasn't arriving.
She turned off the phone to save battery and stared at the ceiling.
No blue glow.
No ambient sounds.
No distractions.

Just… Mira.
And her thoughts.
The next morning was worse.
Still no power. No signal. The city was still asleep, the streets quiet, traffic lights out, stores closed. Mira paced the kitchen, her phone at 23%. She kept checking it like a nervous tick.

"Do you think this is like… serious?" she asked her mom, who was boiling water on the gas stove with matches.

"No one really knows yet," her mom said, stirring instant coffee. "But people are saying the whole grid might've gone down. Like a big systems failure."

"Wait like… the whole city?" Mira asked, eyes wide.

Her mom nodded. "Maybe even more. Could be nationwide. We'll find out when we can."

Mira leaned against the fridge. Her skin itched. Not physically it was more like a hum beneath her bones. An anxiety she couldn't scroll away.

She pulled out her notebook the one she hadn't touched in months and stared at the empty page. Her pen hovered. Nothing came.

She threw it across the room.
By midday, the restlessness turned into frustration. She walked to the corner store closed. No music playing. No buzz of electric doors or debit machines. Just cardboard signs on windows and confused people milling around with dead phones in their hands.

It felt like watching a city hold its breath.
At the park, Mira saw a few people gathered. Kids throwing a frisbee. A woman sketching in a pad. Someone playing a guitar near the fountain.
No one was looking down.
They were looking at each other.
It felt weirdly intimate. Like everyone had forgotten how to do this but were figuring it out together.

Mira sat on a bench; her phone still clutched in her hand even though it was useless now like muscle memory she couldn't undo.

That's when she noticed him.
Evan, from English class.

He was sitting cross-legged under a tree, sketching something in his pad with messy, confident strokes. No earbuds. No phone. Just… him.
Present.
Alive in the moment.

Mira looked away before he could see her watching.

She wanted to say something. Maybe about the silence. Or how weird it felt to not know what was happening online. Or how her skin felt like it was crawling with things she couldn't name.
But she didn't.
Not yet.
That night, the darkness returned like a curtain falling.
No city lights.
No blue glow behind bedroom windows.
No screen to numb her thoughts.
Mira sat on the floor of her room; her knees drawn to her chest. She felt small in a way she hadn't in a long time. Not in a dramatic, poetic way just… real.

Stripped.

She stared at her phone. Battery at 8%. No messages. No new posts. Just her lock screen reflecting her tired face.

She whispered into the dark, “I don’t know how to be without this.”

And the silence whispered nothing back.

Chapter 4 Day One Offline

Withdrawal and unexpected discovery

Mira didn't sleep much. She lay in bed, wrapped in a cocoon of blankets that felt more like a trap than comfort. Her phone sat lifeless beside her pillow. She'd pressed the power button again around 3 a.m., as if it might change its mind. It didn't. No screen. No sound. No glow to keep the dark from pressing in.

The silence was not peaceful. It was invasive too sharp, too loud. Her thoughts, usually muffled by noise and endless scrolling, surged forward like a flood.

What are people doing right now?
What's happening online?
Did anyone try to text me?
Does Evan even know I exist offline?

She flipped onto her back and stared at the ceiling. Her fingers twitched, thumb instinctively mimicking the swipe motion. Scroll. Like. Tap. Refresh. Repeat.

Nothing.

Time crawled.
She finally rolled out of bed, her head heavy. Not the kind of heavy from lack of sleep the kind that came with too much thinking. She shuffled downstairs, socks barely making a sound on the wooden steps.

The kitchen light was dim. A candle flickered near the stove. Her mom was already at the table, hands wrapped around a warm mug, steam curling into the still air.

No music. No news blaring. No phone in sight.

Mira paused in the doorway. Something felt off or maybe real. Like stepping into a dream, she wasn't sure she wanted to wake up in.

"You okay?" her mom asked, her voice gentler than usual.

Mira shrugged, her body moving but her brain still catching up. "Just… weird, I guess."

She opened the fridge, stared at it blankly. She wasn't hungry. She was restless but not the kind of restless that could be fixed by food or a walk or even sleep. It was a phantom itch. A deep, aching need to connect… but all her usual doors were locked.

Her mom gestured to the chair across from her. Mira hesitated, then sat. They didn't speak for a long moment.

"I keep reaching for my phone," Mira mumbled, finally. "Like, every ten minutes. It's like… muscle memory."

"Same," her mom admitted. "I tried to ask Alexa what the weather was this morning. Forgot she's out of commission."

Mira let out a reluctant laugh. It sounded strange in her own ears raw, unfiltered. It felt… human.

She watched her mom sip her coffee, and for the first time in a long time, she noticed her. Not as background noise to her scrolling. Not as an interruption. Just… her mom. Present. Tired. Real.

There was something comforting in the quiet between them uncomfortable too, but not in a bad way. Just unfamiliar.

Later, Mira wandered the house like a ghost. Her phone was still in her pocket a security blanket, even though it was useless. She picked up a book from the shelf, ran her fingers across the spine. Started reading, but the words blurred. Her brain wasn't ready. She tried journaling but couldn't get past the first line. Instead, she sketched swirls and spirals in the margins. The movement soothed her. Like trying to remember how to breathe without being told how.

The day stretched long and slow.

At one point, she just… lay on the floor. The ceiling above her was cracked in one corner. She'd never noticed. A tiny spider was weaving something delicate in the corner of the window frame. The sun poured in, cutting soft lines across the rug.

When was the last time she just looked at sunlight?

Her mom found her like that. "You want to go for a walk?"

Mira blinked. "Outside?"

Her mom nodded, already pulling on a jacket. "Fresh air. Trees. All that analog stuff."

Mira rolled her eyes but got up. The outside world felt alien. Still. Quiet. Neighbors were out, aimless and dazed like her but smiling. Talking. Kids on bikes. An elderly couple sitting on their porch, holding hands.

It felt like stepping into the past. Or maybe a version of the present that had been hiding all along.

As they walked, Mira kept glancing at the sky. It was ridiculously blue. Like cartoon-blue. She felt silly for noticing and even sillier for how much it moved her.

Her chest still felt tight. Her brain still reached for things that weren't there. But in the space left behind, something else began to stir fragile, unfamiliar, but very much alive.

She didn't know what it was yet.
But it felt like the beginning of something.

Chapter 5 Stranger Silence

She visits the park just to be around people. Everyone's outside. Mira sees Evan drawing in a notebook. They start to talk. It's awkward at first but real.

The second day felt less like withdrawal and more like recovery.

Mira's brain still fizzed at the edges, full of phantom pings and invisible notifications. But the panic was gone. Now it was just a low ache like coming down from a sugar rush and realizing how tired you really are.

She wandered outside mid-morning. The house was quiet, too quiet, and the garden's earthy stillness had started to feel like a whisper she couldn't quite understand. She didn't have a destination in mind just the itch to be around life, even if she wasn't ready to talk to it.

The Park was fuller than she'd ever seen it. Not loud not chaotic just alive. A dog barked in the distance. Someone laughed. The breeze rustled the trees in a language older than notifications.

She found herself walking slower, watching everything the cracks in the sidewalk, the way people's eyes met and lingered in a way they never used to. No one was rushing. No one was scrolling.

Then she saw him.

Evan.

He was under the same sycamore tree she passed every day on the way to school, except now she noticed how the branches curved like open arms, like the whole thing was built to hold someone exactly like him.

He didn't see her at first. His head was tilted, eyes narrowed in concentration. His hand moved across a sketchbook with practiced ease, his pencil gliding in slow, confident lines. It wasn't performative. It wasn't for anyone else.

It was quiet joy.

Mira hesitated; feet frozen. She felt like she'd walked into a room where she didn't belong not because she wasn't welcome, but because she hadn't earned it.

But then he looked up.

Their eyes met. Mira’s pulse fluttered.

“Hey,” she said, barely above a whisper.

Evan nodded, the corners of his mouth twitching into a half-smile. “Hey.”

She shifted her weight. “I didn’t mean to interrupt.”

“You didn’t.”

“What are you drawing?” she asked, inching closer. Her voice felt too loud, even though it wasn’t.

He tilted the sketchbook so she could see. A loose portrait not perfect, but full of movement. A woman on a nearby bench, reading a book, her hands expressive even in stillness.

“She’s been flipping that same page for five minutes,” he said. “Like she’s thinking too hard to read.”

Mira blinked. “You notice stuff like that?”

He shrugged. “When there’s nothing else to look at, yeah. People are interesting when they don’t know they’re being watched.”

She nodded, then after a beat, said, “I used to draw too.”

Evan glanced at her, curious but not judgmental. “Used to?”

“I stopped when I got my first phone,” she admitted. “Drawing felt too slow. Too quiet. I didn’t realize I missed it until everything stopped.”

He smiled, soft and understanding. “The quiet can be weird at first. But it’s honest.”

Mira sat down cross-legged in the grass, a few feet away. “You always this… calm?”

Evan chuckled, eyes back on his sketchbook. “God, no. I used to be glued to screens like everyone else. But it made me feel like a ghost. Like I was watching my life from the outside.”

That hit something in Mira’s chest that hollow floaty feeling she never had words for.

“So what changed?” she asked.

“I got sick. A couple years ago. Nothing major, just… enough to knock me offline for a while. Forced break. At first I hated it. Then I realized how much of me I'd been outsourcing to the internet." He paused, looking up. "So I just… didn't go back the same way."

Mira sat with that for a while. It made sense, in a way that hurt a little.

"I don't know who I am without my phone," she whispered, mostly to herself.

Evan didn't try to fix it. He didn't offer a quote or a pep talk. He just kept sketching, letting the silence stretch between them like a bridge instead of a wall.

"You don't have to know yet," he said eventually. "That's the weird part. You get to figure it out."

Mira looked up at the tree branches above them, light filtering through the green like stained glass. Her muscles, clenched for days, finally softened.

It wasn't a grand moment. It wasn't perfect. But it was real.

And for the first time in a long time, that felt like enough.

Chapter 6 No Signal, Just People

More people are coming out neighbors she's never met, old classmates she barely knew. A group of teens, each going through withdrawal in their own way, start hanging out together. They form a strange, screenless bond.

The third day arrived like a slow sunrise not dramatic, not loud, just quietly there.

Mira woke to birdsong, not alarms. A thin strip of golden light touched her wall, warm and honest in a way backlit screen had never been. The craving for her phone still lingered, but it no longer ruled her. She could feel something shifting, like a fog lifting from her brain, one thought at a time.

She ate breakfast with her mom again scrambled eggs, toast, and something unspoken between them that felt like healing. No small talk, no forced conversation. Just presence. It was strange how much space silence had when you let it breathe.

Later, Mira headed outside with no plan, just a pull in her chest that told her: go be around people. It wasn't like her she usually preferred curated company behind glass. But the world had changed. And so, maybe, had she.

The Park was fuller today. Kids ran barefoot across the grass, laughing like the air itself made them drunk. Elderly neighbors chatted on benches; their hands animated with stories. A teen Mira barely recognized from chemistry class was playing an acoustic guitar, fumbling the chords but smiling anyway.

She spotted Evan again under the sycamore tree. He gave a lazy wave, pencil tucked behind his ear. She waved back, but didn't go to him. Not yet.

She wandered deeper into the park, toward the stone amphitheater near the back a place usually empty except during spring concerts. Now, though, a small group had gathered. Teenagers. A few familiar faces, a few unfamiliar. No one was performing. They just sat in a rough circle, legs crossed or sprawled, trading stories, snacks, and long stretches of nothing.

Mira paused at the edge, unsure. But then one girl looked up tall, freckled, with chipped blue nail polish and said, "You can sit if you want."

There was no judgment. No scanning glances. Just invitation.

Mira sat.

At first, she listened. The group was a strange mix quiet, loud, awkward, animated. One guy with a cracked skateboard kept tapping the edge against the concrete like a nervous tic. A girl in a denim jacket kept twisting a braid around her finger. But no one had a phone. No one was performing.

They were just… there.

"So," said the girl with the blue nails, "we were just saying this is like rehab for the internet. Day three. Who's cracked?"

"Me," the skater said immediately. "I keep thinking I'll look something up. Then I remember I can't, and I get angry at trees."

Laughter.

"I tried to text my ex," another girl muttered, face in her hands. "Realized I don't even like him. I just liked texting someone."

More laughter.

Mira found herself smiling. Then, without meaning to, she said, "I've been sleeping better. But I also feel… floaty. Like my brain doesn't know what to hold onto anymore."

Everyone nodded, the kind of nod that says same.

They shared more weird dreams, withdrawal headaches, memories from childhood before phones were everything. Someone mentioned building a garden in the abandoned lot behind the library. Someone else wanted to start a screen-free scavenger hunt. Ideas poured out like they'd been waiting all this time for ears that would really listen.

And Mira noticed something: when someone spoke, everyone looked at them. Not past them. Not through them. At them. Fully.

She'd forgotten what that felt like.

They stayed until the sun dipped low and the shadows grew long, painting the amphitheater in warm amber. Someone started humming a song. Someone else joined in. No one cared about being in tune.

As they parted ways, the girl with the blue nail polish turned to Mira.

“We’ll be back here tomorrow,” she said. “Same time. If you wanna come.”

Mira nodded, heart fuller than she could explain. “Yeah. I’ll come.”

As she walked home, a breeze tugged gently at her hoodie. The city felt alive in a new way not louder, but closer. Less pixelated. More real.

She didn’t miss the screen tonight.
Not even a little.

Chapter 7 Life Without Filters

Mira begins journaling, sketching, and laughing not for content, but because it feels good. The group makes plans to host small events: storytelling nights, walks, even painting murals.

There was something sacred about day four.

Not in a grand, epiphany-filled kind of way but in the way the light came through the window a little softer. In how Mira's body began to settle into the stillness, like it had finally stopped bracing for a ping that would never come.

For the first time in years, she didn't wake up with the pull to check anything. No reflex-swipe. No scroll. Just breath and light and the quiet creak of the house stretching into morning.

She found an old sketchbook buried at the back of her closet the cover frayed, pages curled at the edges. Inside were half-drawn faces, doodles from middle school, pages with notes in the margins like tiny time capsules. Her handwriting had changed. So had she.

Mira sat on her bedroom floor and drew for hours.

At first, it felt rusty the pencil didn't move the way it used to. Her hand cramped. Lines were messy. But then, slowly, the noise in her head thinned out, and something clicked. She stopped trying to make it good. She just made it.

She drew her mother's hands. The sycamore tree in the park. A face that looked suspiciously like Evan's, even though she'd never admit it out loud. Her laughter, when it came, surprised her small and soft and totally unfiltered.

Later that day, she met the group at the amphitheater again. More teens had gathered the circle was growing. There was no leader. No agenda. Just people sharing the shape of their days.

"I started writing poetry again," one girl said, twirling a pen between her fingers. "It's terrible, but I forgot how freeing it is to suck at something and not post it."

"I've been collecting weird rocks," said the skateboard guy. "Don't judge. They're cool."

Someone clapped. Someone else passed around sun-warmed grapes in a plastic container. No one looked at a screen. The world existed only here, in breath and voice and eye contact.

Ideas started to bloom like wildflowers.

"We should host a storytelling night," said Blue Nails. "Just... like, open mic. No phones. No filters."

"What about a walk?" someone offered. "No destination, just people moving together."

"We could paint the underpass near the library. It's always tagged with garbage. Let's make something beautiful."

The ideas tumbled over one another, like kids chasing fireflies. No one shot anything down. No one asked for permission. They just said yes.

Mira felt herself pulled into the current not dragged, but lifted. She told them about her sketchbook. About how she was drawing again.

"You should bring it," Zo said. "Maybe sketch the event. Or help paint."

"Yeah," Mira said, a little surprised by how sure she was. "I'd like that."

They spent the rest of the afternoon sprawled in the grass, planning details on scraps of paper and cardboard. Someone had colored pencils. Someone else had sidewalk chalk. It wasn't perfect, but it was theirs.

Mira walked home with chalk dust on her hands and sun on her cheeks. She passed people on porches, kids on bikes, a woman singing softly to herself as she swept her steps.

Everything looked the same.
But Mira saw it differently now.

She didn't need to share it online to know it mattered. She didn't need a double tap to confirm it was beautiful.

She felt it. Fully.
Without filters.

And that was enough.

Chapter 8 Ghosts of the Feed

A few people can't handle the disconnect and disappear back into their houses. Mira has a dream of her feed swallowing her whole. She starts wondering who she really is without the constant feedback loop.

It began with silence not peaceful this time, but heavy. Thick with something Mira couldn't name.

By day five, the newness had started to wear off. The hum of post-blackout novelty was fading, replaced by a quieter kind of tension. Like everyone was waiting for something to break.

Some of the faces from the group stopped showing up.

"Maybe they're just busy," Zo said, but her tone was thin, unconvinced.

"They're cracking," Evan murmured later, when they walked to the library lot together. "The silence hits different for some people. It gets loud."

Mira understood. More than she wanted to admit.

That night, her sleep came in fragments. She woke twice, sweating, her hand fumbling in the dark for a phone that still wouldn't turn on. By the third time, she gave up and stared at the ceiling, heart racing with no clear reason.

And then came the dream.

She stood in a blank, glowing room. Walls of scrolling content surrounded her fast, endless, pixel-sharp. Familiar voices echoed in comment threads. Notifications blinked like stars. Her own face appeared, again and again, filtered and smiling, looping back on itself.

Her fingers moved without her. Swipe. Double tap. Swipe. Like muscle memory that wasn't hers anymore.

The feed began to close in. The edges tightened. Screens stacked on screens, overlapping like a digital avalanche. Her reflection blurred. Her body disappeared.

Only her profile remained.

And still, the scrolling didn't stop.

She woke up gasping.

Mira sat on the edge of her bed, her chest tight, her mind buzzing with phantom likes. Her hands trembled in the early light. Not from fear — from something deeper. From the realization that part of her still missed it.

The noise. The constant affirmation. The curated chaos.

Who was she without it?

She walked to the mirror and stared at herself really stared. No filter. No ring lights. Just sleep-mussed hair, uneven skin, and eyes full of something raw.

She whispered, “Who are you if no one’s watching?”

There was no answer.

But maybe that was the beginning of one.

Later that afternoon, the group met again, smaller this time. The ones who returned looked tired but clearer like people clawing their way out of a storm.

They didn't talk much. Just shared space. Some wrote in notebooks. Others sketched or watched the clouds.

Mira pulled out her sketchbook but didn't draw. Instead, she watched Zo press wildflowers into the pages of an old book. Evan sat nearby, reading something dog-eared and underlined. For a moment, she felt outside of herself like watching a film that moved slower than real life.

She didn't know if she belonged here forever. But she wanted to.

And that mattered.

As the sun dipped below the horizon, Mira thought of her dream again the endless feed, the vanishing girl, the hollow heart of digital noise.

She looked around at the friends she barely knew a week ago. Real. Tangled. Present.

She whispered to herself again, this time with a little more certainty:
"I'm still here."

And for now, that was enough.

Chapter 9 Confessions

The group shares their struggles social anxiety, depression, cyberbullying, imposter syndrome. Mira tells the truth: she was addicted. She didn't know how to be alone without distraction.

The sun bled into the sky like watercolor, soft purples and pale golds fading into each other as dusk arrived. Mira walked slowly to the lot behind the library, sketchbook in hand, not for drawing this time but just to hold like a tether to something real.

The others were already there. The group was growing smaller again, but something about that made tonight feel more intimate. Evan was seated on an upside-down crate, sketching the worn brick of the library wall. Zo leaned against the old couch with a blanket wrapped around her shoulders, her blue nails chipped nearly to nothing. The others trickled in, no phones, no distractions just a quiet tension that Mira could feel like static in the air.

No one spoke at first. The silence wasn't awkward it was full. Like they all sensed something unspoken had reached the surface and just hadn't broken through yet.

It was Zo who spoke first.

"I used to have a finsta," she said, without preamble. Her voice was low, but clear. "One where I could post my real thoughts. My fears. The ugly stuff I didn't want anyone from school to see."

People shifted, listening, leaning into the quiet like it was holy.

"I posted about feeling invisible. Like, screaming inside invisible. And someone I trusted screenshotted it and turned it into a meme. Sent it around."

No one interrupted.

"I laughed it off. Pretended I didn't care. Then I deleted the account. Deleted everything. I thought that would make me feel better, but honestly… I think the silence after hurt even more. Like I'd erased myself."

She looked down, blinked fast, then smiled a little, without humor. “Anyway. That’s mine.”

Silence.

Then the boy in the gray hoodie Nico spoke. “I used to schedule posts. Like, legit, plan when to be funny, or deep, or hot. It was all strategy. I wasn’t a person. I was a brand.”

A small laugh from someone. Not mocking understanding.

He shrugged. “It messed with my head. I’d delete stuff if it didn’t hit fast enough. I stopped saying what I meant. I just said what worked.”

Another girl chimed in Yasmin, her hair up in a messy bun, eyes rimmed red. “I got cyberbullied in middle school for wearing the same hoodie in two selfies. One comment turned into fifty. They called me homeless Barbie. I didn’t wear that hoodie for two years after that. It was my favorite one.”

Someone reached out and touched her arm gently. No words. Just warmth.

Evan looked up from his sketchbook but didn’t speak right away. He just looked at the sky, then said, “I never had socials. Everyone thought I was weird. But it was because I knew myself too well, I would've gotten sucked in. I have an addictive brain."

He smiled, not proud, not ashamed just honest.

Then came Mira's turn. She could feel the silence shift toward her, not in pressure, but invitation. The kind that waits for you to step into your truth.

She looked down at her hands, at the faint pencil smudges on her skin from earlier, and said, "I used to scroll… everywhere."

Her voice cracked, so she paused and let it settle.

"Like, not just boredom scrolling. It was always. On the toilet. In bed. In class. During dinner. I'd wake up and check Instagram before I even said a word to my mom."

A hush. Not judgment reverence.

"My brain needed noise. I didn't know how to just be without it. Even when I hated what I saw online, I kept going back. Like it was filling some hole I couldn't name."

She met their eyes, one by one.

"I think I was addicted. And I didn't know how to stop. Until the blackout, I didn't even realize how far I'd gone."

Her voice broke again. This time, she didn't fight it.

"I was scared to be alone. Not physically. I was scared to be alone with my thoughts."

Silence again, deep and full. Mira felt raw, but not exposed more like uncovered.

Zo leaned forward. "That's real," she said softly. "Thank you."

Yasmin nodded. "It's crazy how we all felt like this, but never said it."

Evan closed his sketchbook. "We couldn't. The internet's too loud to hear anything real."

They stayed long after the light left the sky, after streetlights flickered on, after the wind started to nip at their sleeves.

The circle was quiet, but something had changed. Something inside it had solidified not just a group of kids hiding from a digital world, but a constellation of stories, stitched together by honesty.

Before they broke for the night, someone whispered, “We should keep this going. This… space.”

No one disagreed.

Mira walked home feeling lighter and heavier all at once. She hadn’t fixed anything. But she’d told the truth.

And the truth had landed. Not on a screen, but in hearts.

That was more than she’d ever expected.

Chapter 10 Creating Something Real

The group decides to build something together a community garden, a pop-up art wall, something physical. Mira leads a project to write "letters to your future self."

The idea didn't come from one person. It came from the air between them from silence made sacred, from stories whispered under a sky without notifications.

They were tired of only talking. Of just sitting and remembering who they were. They needed to make something. To touch it. To plant it. To leave it behind.

"We should build something," Nico said, kicking a loose stone in the lot. "Not for likes. Just… for us."

Mira's pulse ticked up. She didn't know why yet, but that sentence did something to her.

Zo sat forward; her fingers stained from ink. "Like what?"

“Could be a mural,” Yasmin said. “We’ve got that old wall near the underpass. The city doesn’t care what happens there it’s all just tags and grime.”

Evan looked thoughtful. “We could do a garden too. That dead strip of grass by the rec center? It could use some life.”

Ideas spiraled not like wild sparks this time, but like roots twisting downward. This wasn’t about novelty. It was about grounding something. About permanence.

But it was Mira who added the thing that no one else had said yet.

“What if we wrote letters,” she said, voice soft, “to our future selves?”

Everyone looked at her.

“Not for the internet. Not even for each other. Just… to be opened later. Like, months or a year from now. When we forget who we were without the noise.”

Zo traced a fingertip along the frayed hem of her jeans. “It’s like… we’re writing proof that we existed. I’m in.”

“Could be part of the mural,” Evan added. “We seal them behind it. Time capsule style.”

The group lit up not loud, not over the top, but with quiet nods and glances that said, yes. This.

They spent the next few days planning, scavenging, collecting paint from storage rooms and borrowing tools from forgotten sheds. Nico’s older brother brought shovels. Yasmin biked three miles to a garden shop and came back with seed packets and dirt-streaked joy.

Mira found herself in motion again. But this time, not as a background scroll or filtered face as someone real, someone doing. She drafted letter prompts. She cut sheets of brown paper from grocery bags. She borrowed a stapler from her mom without asking and tucked it into her backpack like treasure.

On the third day, they stood before the wall.

It was gray and cracked and ugly perfect.

They cleaned it together, scraping off old graffiti, scrubbing grime until their arms ached. No music played. No selfies were taken. Just sweat and laughter and the kind of conversation that flowed without structure.

The mural wasn't designed it grew. Every person added something: colors, symbols, fragments of poems. Evan drew a girl floating between two worlds. Zo painted a hand reaching out of static. Yasmin scrawled; we were never alone just unplugged.

And Mira she wrote her letter.

Dear Future Me,
I used to be scared of silence. Now I know it's where I find myself.
I hope you still remember how it felt to be here.
Not scrolling. Not performing. Just alive.
Love,
Mira

She folded it, sealed it with tape, and pressed it behind the wall with the others. Then they layered over it paint, handprints, stars, lines of gold.

The past covered in color. The future hidden inside.

When they stepped back, the mural looked like a confession and a prayer all at once. Not perfect. Not polished. But theirs.

That night, Mira stood at the edge of the garden they'd just begun to dig. The soil was uneven, but full of promise. Like all of them.

"I feel like we planted something inside ourselves too," Zo said, handing Mira a trowel. "Like… memory."

Mira smiled.

"Yeah," she said. "And maybe a way forward."

Chapter 11 Power Returns

The blackout ends. Everything comes back online. Phones light up. People scatter. Mira is tempted. The group chat buzzes. She stares at her screen… but doesn't touch it.

It started with a hum.

Mira heard it before she saw anything the low, electric sigh of the city exhaling all at once.

The light in her bedroom blinked once, then glowed steady. Down the hall, the refrigerator groaned back to life. Across the street, a TV buzzed loud, laughter spilling out of an open window like it had never left.

Power was back.

She stared at the ceiling, half-buried under a tangle of blankets, and felt the weight of it hit her in waves not relief. Not joy. Just… noise. Returning.

Downstairs, her mom let out a quiet "thank God" and fiddled with the Wi-Fi router. Mira didn't move. Her phone sat on her desk across the room lifeless, still, silent for days. For a heartbeat, it looked like a relic. Then, slowly, the screen flickered on.

Buzz.
Buzz.
Buzz.

Like it had been holding its breath, waiting.

Notifications poured in, cascading down the lock screen in a flood of missed texts, app alerts, group chat pings, algorithmic invitations to reenter the feed.

Mira stayed frozen.

She thought about the mural. The garden. The laughter around the fire pit. Evan sketching wildflowers into the dirt. Zo singing softly as they painted over rust. The sound of Yasmin reading her letter out loud and crying halfway through.

She thought about silence how loud it had been at first. And how necessary it became.

Buzz.

Her screen lit again: Group Chat – 117 Messages.

She crossed the room and picked up the phone.

The weight of it felt familiar, like a reflex slipping back into place. Her thumb hovered above the screen. She didn't unlock it.

Instead, she stared at her reflection in the black mirror between notifications. Her own eyes clearer than she remembered.

Downstairs, the Wi-Fi connected. Music played. Her mom sighed with relief again. The neighborhood pulsed with life screens lighting up behind windows, voices overlapping with digital sound. A hundred homes reactivating at once.

Mira breathed in.
Held it.
Let it go.

She clicked the power button.

The screen went dark again.

And this time, it stayed off.

Later that afternoon, the group met in their usual place the mural now fully dry, catching golden light like a stained-glass memory.

Some didn't show. Some had already returned to their old habits, lured back by the glow.

But a few came. Evan. Zo. Yasmin. Nico. Mira.

They didn't say much at first. Just stood there, watching the wall.

"Power's back," Nico said.

"Yeah," Evan replied. "But we don't have to be."

Zo pulled out a worn notebook, flipping to a page she'd scribbled on during the blackout. "We should keep meeting. Not just 'til this wears off. Like… actually keep it going. Even if we're the only ones."

Mira nodded slowly.

"What if we make it official?" she spoke. "A screen-free space. Saturdays. Here."

Everyone looked at her.

"You'd lead it?" Evan asked.

Mira hesitated not out of fear, but because she knew what saying yes would mean.

She smiled. “Yeah. I think I would.”

The city buzzed in the distance. Notifications multiplied in the air like pollen.

But here, in this space between power and presence, something real remained.

Chapter 12 Choosing Connection

Mira and her new friends meet intentionally and decide to stay connected, offline. They create a weekly screen-free hangout. She deletes half her apps.

The power was back. The noise was back.

But Mira didn't rush into it this time.

Her phone sat in her backpack for two whole days, untouched. When she finally opened it, it didn't feel like a lifeline it felt like a tool. One she could choose not to use.

The group met again the following Saturday, just as they'd promised, beneath the half-finished garden sign painted in messy strokes of green and orange:
Offline & Alive.

It was Yasmin who suggested the name. Evan carved it into the wooden edge of the raised garden bed, slow and careful.

More people came this time. Not a flood but a few. Some from school. One kid from Zo's bus stop. A younger girl Mira had seen crying alone in the lunchroom once. They brought snacks, notebooks, guitars. One kid read poetry under the tree near the mural. Someone else played a quiet chord progression on an out-of-tune keyboard.

No one checked their phone.

Not once.

It wasn’t a rule just a rhythm.

Mira passed around slips of paper with simple prompts:
Something you’re proud of.
A fear you let go of this week.
Something real that happened to you, not your screen.

People wrote. People read. People laughed.

It was so quiet; you could hear the leaves whispering.

Later that night, back in her room, Mira stared at her phone. The icons were all there, lined up like little doorways. She’d visited every one of them a thousand times.

Her thumb hovered over them, one by one.

Delete.
Delete.
Keep.
Delete.
Pause notifications.
Turn off badges.
Goodbye, TikTok.
Goodbye, curated self.

She kept her camera. She liked taking pictures of things that didn't need sharing cracked sidewalks, clouds, her mom's hands when she made chai.

She kept texts. Real messages, with real people.

And she kept the notes app it was filled with words she hadn't had the courage to say out loud until recently.

When she was done, her phone looked… empty.

And she felt full.

The next morning, Mira printed flyers:
Screen-Free Saturdays – Behind the Library –
Music. Murals. Real Life.
She handed them out in homeroom. Taped one to the back of a bathroom stall. Left one in the

principal's mailbox with a handwritten note: It's helping. Please don't shut it down.

That day, she walked the halls without her phone in her hand. Her head was up. Her shoulders open.

Someone smiled at her a real smile, not an emoji.

She smiled back.

Chapter 13 Letters and Light

Mira reads the letter she wrote to herself on Day 3. She cries. Her relationship with her mom heals. She starts writing zines and even starts a "Screen-Free Saturday" movement at her school.

The sky was pale lavender, soft and slanted with late afternoon light. The mural caught it like glass, glowing faintly where the sun met gold paint. Mira stood in front of it, heart thudding as she peeled back a panel a secret slit just wide enough to reach into the hollow space behind the wall.

The letters were still there.

She recognized her own by the shape of the fold, the way she'd torn the edge of the paper unevenly, like her hands hadn't been steady that day.

She sat on the grass and unfolded it with slow fingers. Her heart clenched.

Dear Future Me,
I used to be scared of silence. Now I know it's where I find myself.
I hope you still remember how it felt to be here.
Not scrolling. Not performing. Just alive.

Love,
Mira.

She didn't expect to cry but she did.

Not because she was sad.

Because she recognized the girl who had written those words, and for the first time in a long time, she didn't want to change her. She just wanted to sit beside her and say: You made it.

That night, Mira found her mom in the kitchen, stirring lentils and humming softly to herself.

Mira leaned against the counter and said, "I read the letter."

Her mom turned, surprise softening into something gentler. "The one you wrote during the blackout?"

Mira nodded. "It made me realize I want to keep doing this. Living like this."

Her mom smiled not with relief, but with pride. "You've changed," she said quietly.

"So have we," Mira said. "Together."

They ate dinner without the TV. Without their phones. Just voices and real presence, the kind that made the silence feel full instead of empty.

The next morning, Mira opened a blank notebook and started to write not journaling, not venting, but building something. She created her first zine: Unfiltered. Hand-drawn pages. Snippets of poems. Tiny manifestos in the margins. One issue became two, then five. She left them in the library. In lockers. On benches.

And kids started reading them.

Not everyone got it. But the ones who did? They felt it.

The next Saturday, Mira stood in front of twenty students in the art room after school, holding a hand-painted sign:
SCREEN-FREE SATURDAYS
Real talk. Real life. Real you.

She didn't speak like a leader. She spoke like a person.

"Technology isn't the enemy," she told them. "But losing ourselves in it — that's the risk. This space is just a way to remember who we are without the noise."

Heads nodded. Shoulders relaxed.

She passed out paper. Pens. Tea in mismatched mugs. Music played low in the background a record, not a playlist.

Someone whispered, “This feels like breathing.”

And Mira?
She smiled.
Because it did.

Chapter 14 Real Life (Not Live)

A year later. The city is glowing with screens again, but Mira is different. She uses tech mindfully, shares her story, and helps others struggling with digital addiction.

The city didn't change.

It still glowed. Still buzzed. Still whispered promises through notifications, trends, filters, loops.

But Mira had changed.

Not all at once. Not in some dramatic, irreversible way. But slowly. Intentionally. Like learning to breathe again after holding it in too long.

She still had a phone. She still took pictures sometimes even posted them. But she no longer felt like she had to be on all the time. She didn't feel hollow after scrolling. She noticed that shift the difference between using tech and being used by it.

She had learned the texture of her own attention. How fragile it was. How beautiful.

Every morning, she started with a screen-free hour. Sometimes she journaled. Sometimes she made tea and just… stared out the window. That alone used to terrify her. Now it felt like her anchor.

At school, she launched Digital Quiet, a space for anyone who felt overwhelmed. It was held in the library every Wednesday no agenda, no judgment. Just a circle of students, a warm light, and the quiet permission to not perform.

Some came to write. Some cried. Some just sat.

Mira always brought paper and pens. Clay for sculpting. Old magazines for blackout poetry. She played vinyl records sometimes not for the aesthetic, but because it forced everyone to listen.

The posters she'd made read:
The first meeting had four people.
The fourth had sixteen.

One girl Hailey, a freshman stayed behind after a session once and whispered, "I didn't know quiet could be this loud."

Mira just smiled. She understood.

Outside school, Screen-Free Saturdays had turned into a small movement. Kids who once couldn't go ten minutes without checking their phones now hosted mural nights, community clean-ups, even a little flea market where everything was made by hand zines, bracelets, linocut prints.

Mira had become something unexpected. Not an influencer. Not a leader.

A mirror.
Just someone reflecting what could be possible.

She still met with Evan most weekends. Sometimes in the garden, sometimes just walking through neighborhoods with no destination. He still didn't have any social media. He carried a sketchbook everywhere and drew people when they didn't notice faces half-turned, soft smiles, the curve of someone's fingers holding a coffee cup.

"You notice the world more when you're not trying to capture it," he'd said once, his pencil barely moving.

Zo ran her own workshop now Creative Mess Club, where people could paint with their hands and get their clothes dirty. Yasmin wrote essays and read them aloud in poetry slams. Nico started writing songs again.

Mira stayed soft through it all.

There were still days she felt the pull the itch to scroll, to disappear, to compare. Sometimes she gave in. But now, she noticed. She forgave. And she came back.

That was the difference.

At home, things had softened too. Her mom no longer yelled from the other room when she wanted to talk, she came and sat beside Mira. They cooked together. Mira taught her how to make a zine once her mom glued pressed flowers to the cover and titled it Things, I Never Said but Should Have.

That one made Mira cry.
On the anniversary of the blackout, Mira went to the rooftop with her letter again the one she had written to herself. She brought a candle. A mug of mint tea. Her notebook.
The city below flickered like a galaxy of attention spans.
She reread the letter, then wrote a new one.

Chapter 15 When the Pixel Fades

Final reflection. Mira's voice, hopeful and grounded. She learned that connection isn't found in pixels it's found in presence. The last line: "This isn't the end. This is where it really begins."

The glow is still there.

In windows. In pockets. In palms. In streets painted with LED billboards and banner ads that flash like modern prayers: Watch this. Want this. Be this.

But I'm not pulled under anymore.

When the pixel fades when the brightness goes out and the noise quiets what's left?

That used to terrify me. The stillness. The self beneath it all.

But now I know: what's left is me.

Not the filtered version, not the digital echo, not the girl who crafted captions to feel seen.
Just… Mira.
Breathing. Listening. Choosing.

I still use tech. I still scroll sometimes. I text. I watch the occasional reel of some dog wearing tiny sunglasses. It makes me laugh.
But I don't vanish into it anymore.
I stay with myself.
And I stay with others, too. Not just liking their highlight reels, but witnessing the pauses between their sentences. The way someone's voice shakes when they speak the truth. The quiet kind of courage it takes to be real.

Presence. That's the word I keep returning to.

Not performance. Not perfection. Presence.

It lives in held eye contact. In dirt under fingernails from planting something that will take months to grow. In laughter that spills out during shared silences. In stories whispered at dusk on folding chairs and cracked pavement.

I carry that presence now like a lantern.

And when I feel myself slipping again when the scroll becomes the sedative I return to the candlelight. The letter. The rooftop sky.

And I remember what I learned when everything went dark:

We were never meant to live lit by pixels alone.

We were built for touch. For time. For messy, breathing, unfinished connection.

I don't know exactly who I'll be next year, or five years from now. But I know this:

She won't need to perform to feel worthy.

She'll know where to go when she forgets.
She'll remember the garden.
The zines.
The silence.
The people who chose to stay, even when the feed came back.
And she'll find her way home again.
Because this isn't the end.

This is where it really begins.
She folded it gently. Lit a second candle beside the first.
And let the glow be enough.

www.ingramcontent.com/pod-product-compliance
Ingram Content Group UK Ltd.
Pitfield, Milton Keynes, MK11 3LW, UK
UKHW041347190726
13845UKWH00026B/473

9 789334 279375